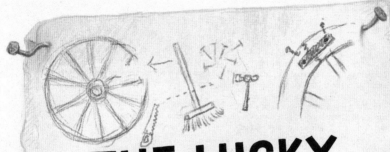

THE LUCKY
WHEEL

By Grace Gilmore
Illustrated by Petra Brown

NEW YORK **NEW DELHI**

I want to thank my wonderful editor, Sonali Fry.

I also want to thank the History Center in Tompkins County for their invaluable assistance in my research.

— G. G.

LITTLE SIMON
An imprint of Simon & Schuster Children's Publishing Division
1230 Avenue of the Americas, New York, New York 10020
This Little Simon edition April 2015
Copyright © 2015 by Simon & Schuster, Inc.
Illustrations by Petra Brown
Designed by Chani Yammer
All rights reserved, including the right of reproduction in whole or in part in any form.
LITTLE SIMON is a registered trademark of Simon & Schuster, Inc., and associated colophon is a trademark of Simon & Schuster, Inc.
For information about special discounts for bulk purchases, please contact
Simon & Schuster Special Sales at 1-866-506-1949 or business@simonandschuster.com.
The Simon & Schuster Speakers Bureau can bring authors to your live event. For more information or to book an event, contact the Simon & Schuster Speakers Bureau at 1-866-248-3049 or visit our website at www.simonspeakers.com.
Manufactured in the United States of America 0315 FFG
10 9 8 7 6 5 4 3 2 1
Library of Congress Cataloging-in-Publication Data
Gilmore, Grace. The lucky wheel / by Grace Gilmore ; illustrated by Petra Brown. — First Little Simon paperback edition. pages cm. — (Tales from Maple Ridge ; [2])
Summary: Each student in Maple Ridge is asked to contribute fifty cents for much needed repairs to the school but Logan has no money, so he decides to sell the buggy wheel he found by the side of the road and carefully fixed, if only he can find a buyer for a single wheel. [1. Repairing—Fiction. 2. Fund raising—Fiction. 3. Family life—Fiction. 4. Farm life—Fiction.] I. Brown, Petra, illustrator. II. Title. PZ7.G4372Luc 2015 [Fic]—dc23
2014010528
ISBN 978-1-4814-2627-5 (pbk)   ISBN 978-1-4814-2628-2 (hc)   ISBN 978-1-4814-2629-9 (eBook)

CONTENTS

CHAPTER 1

A BIG ANNOUNCEMENT

It was Monday morning, and Logan Pryce was late for school.

He ran through the door, out of breath. His knickers and boots were muddy. The other students were already at their desks. Everyone turned and stared at him, including his sister Tess and his older brother, Drew.

Tess mouthed the words, *Where were you?*

Their teacher, Miss Ashley, glanced up from her roll-call sheet. A vase of daffodils sat on her desk,

next to her inkwell and feathery quill pen. "Oh, there you are, Logan. I was about to mark you as absent."

"I'm sorry, Miss Ashley!" said Logan, plucking a dried-up leaf

out of his messy blond hair. "I was on my way inside with the others. Then I spotted a broken button that I thought I could use in my Fix-It

Shop. I was about it pick it up when I slipped and fell in a puddle, and—"

"What is a Fix-It Shop?" Miss Ashley asked.

"My Fix-It Shop is where I fix old things and invent new things!" Logan said proudly.

Miss Ashley smiled at Logan's answer. "That sounds very interesting. In the future, though, please be more mindful of the time.

You may take your seat now." She added, "Class, please face forward!"

The children turned in their seats. The boys sat on one side, and the girls sat on the other. The six- and seven-year-olds sat up front near Miss Ashley.

Drew, who was eleven, sat in the

back with the older
kids. Logan, who
was eight, and Tess,
who was nine, sat
in the middle.

Usually, there
were twenty
students present
in the one-room
schoolhouse. But
spring was planting
season, so a few
of the boys were
missing. Farmers
usually kept their

oldest sons at home to help with the plowing and sowing. Pa used to keep Drew home for this reason.

"I have an announcement to make," Miss Ashley began. "As you can see, our school is overdue for some repairs."

Logan looked around. Three of the floorboards had split and buckled. A breeze whistled through a cracked window. A large hole gaped in the ceiling across from the bookshelves. The walls needed fresh paint.

"I will try to find volunteers to do the repairs," Miss Ashley continued. "But first, we have to raise ten dollars to buy lumber and other supplies. So I need each of you to bring in fifty cents by next Monday."

Fifty cents?

Logan added up the numbers. Fifty cents from

him plus Tess plus Drew equaled a
dollar fifty total.

Their family couldn't afford that
kind of money!

•LOGAN TELLS A LIE•

That night, the Pryces sat down to dinner: Pa, Ma, Drew, Tess, Logan, and little Annie. The family dog, Skeeter, crouched at Logan's feet and chewed on a piece of hide. The kitchen was warm from the cookstove, and the kerosene lamp cast plenty of light. Outside, the first stars twinkled in the sky.

Ma had prepared turnips, carrots, and other vegetables from the root cellar. The first spring crops, like spinach and asparagus, wouldn't be ready for a while.

Canned beets from last fall and freshly baked bread were also on the table.

"Mrs. Wigglesworth doesn't like beets," Annie complained, cradling her doll. "They make her mouth turn terribly red!"

"Well, Mrs. Wigglesworth doesn't have to eat the beets. But you do,"

15

Pa told her. "So how was school today?" he asked the other children.

"Fine," said Drew.

"Fine," said Tess.

"Fine," said Logan.

Pa laughed. "Okay. But what did you learn? Arithmetic? Geography?"

"The advanced group studied science," Drew replied. "That means 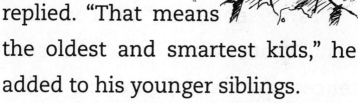 the oldest and smartest kids," he added to his younger siblings.

Logan and Tess made secret, scrunched-up faces at each other. They did this whenever Drew was being annoying.

"Miss Ashley also asked me to help some of the kids parse sentences," Drew went on.

"What are parsley sentences?" asked Annie, who was four and didn't go to school yet.

"Parse sentences," Ma corrected her. "That's when you take sentences apart and figure out which words are action words, which words are things-and-people words, and so on."

Pa smiled at Annie. "You'll learn when you go to school someday, honey. Isn't that right, Alice?" he said to Ma.

"That's right, Dale," Ma agreed.

Logan ate some beets as he listened to the dinner conversation. They were sweet and earthy and made him think of harvesttime on their farm.

Except that their farm was no more. Just last month, Pa had decided to stop being a farmer because he couldn't make enough money

growing crops. He was trying to find steady work in the city of Sherman, near Maple Ridge. In the meantime, he was earning a few dollars here and there doing odd jobs.

"What else happened at school today?" asked Ma as she sliced the bread. "Anything interesting?"

Logan looked nervously at Drew and Tess. He wondered which one would bring up the business of the fifty cents.

But neither of them did. Drew started talking about something called "electricity." Tess cut up Annie's beets for her.

It was up to Logan.

"Miss Ashley said we each have to bring in fifty cents for school repairs," he blurted out.

"I already have my fifty cents. From my birthday money," Tess spoke up.

"Me too." Drew reached for the water pitcher. "I earned fifty cents by hauling hay for

Mr. Gruen. What about you, Logan? You must have money in your piggy bank, right?"

Everyone stared at Logan and waited for his answer.

"Sure I do," Logan mumbled.

"That's wonderful, son," Pa said, patting him on the back. "I'm so proud of all of you for using your own money to help your school."

Logan squirmed. He didn't feel good at all.

He had just told a big, fat lie. His piggy bank—Percy the Pig—was empty.

How was he going to come up with fifty cents in the next seven days?

THE BAD-LUCK DAY

The next day, gray clouds churned in the sky as the Pryce children walked home from school. Logan lifted his face and felt a raindrop. Then another.

"Rain!" he announced to Drew and Tess.

"Just our luck," Drew grumbled. "Of course, none of us brought our

umbrellas or our slickers."

"Maybe Pa will come get us in the buggy," said Logan hopefully. It was a mile back to their house.

"That's not likely. Pa's seeing

Mr. Dawson about a job today," Drew remarked.

"Mr. Dawson? Who's that?" asked Logan.

"He's a newspaperman from Sherman," Drew replied.

"He's starting a weekly paper here in Maple Ridge. He needs extra hands to help him move into his new office."

"Oh, I do hope Pa gets the job!" Tess said eagerly. "He hasn't worked in a while—not since he built that fence for Mr. Kranz's goats."

Drew turned up the collar of his jacket. "At least we didn't have to ask him and Ma for money for the school repairs. I gave my fifty cents to Miss Ashley this morning."

"I'm going to bring mine in tomorrow," said Tess as she tied a big scarf over her long brown braids. "What about you, Logan?"

Logan stared at his boots and said nothing. He pulled his lunch pail onto his head like a hat. Raindrops plinked against the metal and echoed sharply in his ears: *plink, plink, plink.*

Tess tapped him on the arm. "Hello?"

"I don't have it," Logan whispered.

"What did you say?" asked Drew.

"I don't have it," Logan repeated, more loudly. "I lied last night.

Percy the Pig is empty."

"Oh, Logan!" said Tess. She thought for a moment. "Well, I have a nickel left in my piggy bank. You can have it. But you'd still need forty-five cents."

"I have a nickel too," Drew offered.

"Wow, thanks!" Logan took his lunch pail off his head. "Now I just have to find a way to make forty cents."

"Maybe you could sell something from your Fix-It Shop?" Tess said. "One of your great inventions!"

Logan mulled this over. "Hmm, maybe."

Just then they

spotted Skeeter up ahead. He waited for them by the side of the road just past the Pritchetts' apple orchard. He seemed to be sniffing something.

"What is it, boy? What did you find?" Logan called out.

Skeeter barked. Logan, Tess, and Drew began to run. Their boots slogged in the mud forming on the winding country road. Birds

fluttered out of bushes and flew away.

Skeeter stood over an abandoned buggy wheel. It lay in a patch of milkweed and Queen Anne's lace.

The rim and one of the spokes was broken. The wood was scratched up, but still solid.

"Skeeter! This is just what I needed!" Logan exclaimed.

Skeeter wagged his tail. Tess and Drew looked puzzled.

Logan grinned from ear to ear. The bad-luck day had just turned into a good-luck day!

CHAPTER 4

○ FIXING THE WHEEL ○

The next morning, Logan woke up earlier than usual. It was pitch-black outside as he headed to the barn. A sliver of moon lingered in the sky. The air was clear and cold, and he could see his breath. Skeeter trotted along beside him, alert for raccoons and opossums.

In the barn, Logan raced through

his usual chores. First, he milked the cows. Next, he brushed the horses, Lightning and Buttercup, and mucked their stalls too.

When his chores were done, he got to work in his Fix-It Shop. The shop took up one corner of the barn.

A worktable, a chair, and some crates were its only furniture.

The broken wheel sat on the side of Logan's worktable. He picked it up and studied it.

He had a plan.

First, he would have to replace the damaged spoke. Then he would mend the rim. Finally, he would sand the whole thing down to make it smooth. When the wheel was finished, he would sell it to someone for forty cents. He would give the money to Miss Ashley next Monday along

with the two nickels from Tess and Drew.

Logan was eager to get started. He reached down and began digging through his crates. They were filled with a hodgepodge of odd and discarded items like broom handles and copper lids.

There! He spotted a spoke made of sturdy oak. With a little trimming, it would fit his wheel just right. It was a different color from the rest of the wheel, though. A *coat of paint might do the trick,* Logan thought.

But what about the rim? Logan didn't have a spare one in his crate. And he had no clue how to repair the splintered wood.

The barn doors burst open. Drew walked in.

"There you are, Logan. We'll be late for school!"

"What?" Logan had lost track of the time.

Drew glanced at the wheel. "Are you really fussing over that old thing?"

"It'll be good as new when I'm done with it," said Logan abruptly.

"You know, no one is going to buy just one

wheel. You need four matching ones. Unless you've invented a one-wheeled buggy?" Drew joked.

Logan's cheeks grew hot. "Someone will buy it," he insisted.

Someone has to buy it, he thought.

CHAPTER 5

ANTHONY'S BRIGHT IDEA

"I am pleased to report that we have already raised seven dollars for our school repairs," Miss Ashley announced in class, "thanks to those of you who have brought in your money. I am still waiting on contributions from six more students."

"I'll have mine next Monday,

Miss Ashley!" Anthony Bruna spoke up. He was Logan's best friend. "My pa collects his pay from the factory on Fridays."

Miss Ashley turned to Logan. "What about you, Logan? Will you have your money in by Monday too?"

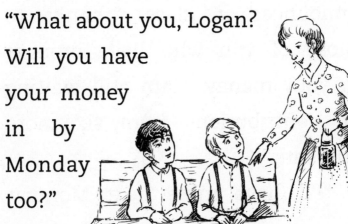

"Yes, Miss Ashley," replied Logan. "I'm fixing up a broken buggy wheel to sell."

In the back of the room, a couple of boys snickered. Tess whirled around and glared at them.

"Kyle! Lenny! That will be quite enough," Miss Ashley scolded.

"Pay no attention to them," Tess whispered to Logan.

Logan shrugged and tried to act like he couldn't care less about Kyle Chambers and Lenny Watts. It wasn't easy, though. Those boys could be pretty mean sometimes.

The rest of the morning flew by. Miss Ashley split the class up into groups. The oldest students helped the youngest students with

their penmanship. Logan, Tess, and Anthony did subtraction. Miss Ashley worked on spelling with the rest of the children.

At lunchtime, Anthony and Logan sat outside together. They

discussed Logan's wheel project
as they ate their bread and hard-
boiled eggs.

"I can't figure out how to mend
the rim," Logan told his friend.

"Gosh, what's wrong with it?" asked Anthony.

"Allow me to demonstrate!"

Logan twisted his cloth napkin and made a circle with it. Then he

made the circle come apart. "It's cracked, like this. I'm not sure how to put it back together again," he explained.

Anthony nodded slowly. "I think I have the answer to your problem."

"You do?"

"Yeah. It's a recipe that my mama makes."

Logan frowned. How in the world could Mrs. Bruna's famous meatballs fix his wheel . . . or her pickled vegetables . . . or her spaghetti with tomato sauce?

"I'm talking about glue," Anthony said with a laugh. "I'll bring you the recipe tomorrow!

CHAPTER 6

○LOGAN CONFESSES○

That night, Logan was finishing up with the spoke when Pa came into the barn.

"Hi, Pa!" Logan greeted him. "What are you doing here?"

"I wanted to look in on Buttercup. She scraped her leg while we were in town today," replied Pa.

Logan glanced over at the golden

mare. "Will she be okay?"

"I put some ointment on the wound. She'll be good as new soon." Pa nodded at Logan's worktable. "You're up awfully late, son. What's keeping you so busy?"

"I found this wheel by the side of the road. I'm fixing it up to sell it," replied Logan.

"I see. Do you have a buyer in mind?"

"Nope. I need to come up with one, though." Logan hesitated. "By Monday."

"Why Monday?" asked Pa curiously.

Logan looked away. "Pa, I lied about having fifty cents in my piggy bank," he confessed.

"Logan Dale Pryce!" said Pa sharply. He and Ma often used Logan's full name when they were angry with him. "You know very well that lying is wrong. Why didn't you just tell us the truth?"

"I'm sorry, Pa! But I didn't want to have to ask you and Ma for the money. So I pretended that I had it."

Pa frowned and was quiet for a couple minutes. To Logan, it felt like forever.

"You can always come to us, son," he said finally.

"Yes, Pa."

"We're a family. We solve all of our problems together."

"Yes, Pa."

"Have you thought about Mr. Mayberry at the general store? He might be interested in buying your wheel. He could then resell it to one of his customers for a profit."

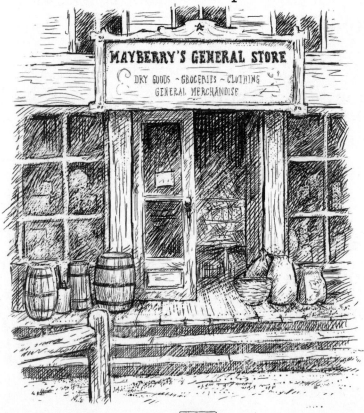

"That's a swell idea, Pa!" Logan exclaimed. "Except . . . what's a profit?"

"A profit means making money," Pa told him. "If you sell it to Mr. Mayberry for forty cents, you make a profit of forty cents. If he resells it to someone else for a dollar, he makes a profit of sixty cents."

Logan nodded. Pa made a lot of sense.

"Thanks, Pa," he said softly.

Pa squeezed Logan's shoulder. "You're welcome, son."

CHAPTER 7

◦ COOKING GLUE ◦

The following evening, Logan sat at the kitchen table and studied Mrs. Bruna's glue recipe. Anthony had given it to him at school. It was in Mrs. Bruna's nice handwriting and said:

A RECIPE FOR GLUE

Please make sure that your mama or papa helps you with this task!

Please make sure that your mama or papa helps you with this task!

1. Mix one cup flour and one~third cup sugar in a small pan.

2. Add three~quarters cup water and mix into a paste.

3. Add another three~quarters cup water and mix some more.

4. Add one teaspoon vinegar.

5. Cook until the glue starts to become thick.

6. Cool and store in a jar.

Ma and Tess read the recipe over Logan's shoulder. "We have all the ingredients," said Ma after a

moment. "Tess, can you fetch the flour, sugar, and vinegar?"

"Yes, Ma." Tess retrieved two metal canisters and a glass bottle from the pantry.

"Do we have a measuring cup?" Logan asked Ma.

"We sure do!" Ma reached into the cupboard and pulled out a tin cup with numbers on it.

Logan and Tess measured the flour, sugar, and other ingredients and poured them into a cast-iron pan. Ma set the pan on the stove and stirred the mixture with a wooden spoon.

While the glue cooked, Logan
and Tess washed up the dinner
dishes. They used a big pot of water
that Ma had heated on the stove.
The house was still and peaceful.
Drew was in the boys' room doing
his homework.
Skeeter lay
on the

kitchen floor and chomped on a bone. Annie was asleep, and so was Pa. Logan knew that Pa was tired from moving furniture for Mr. Dawson, the newspaperman, all day.

When the glue was done, Logan and Tess poured it into a glass jar.

"Why don't we put the jar outside for the night?"

Ma suggested. "The temperature is colder than it is in the house, so the glue will cool faster."

"Good idea!" said Logan.

"I hope the glue will help you with your wheel project," Ma added.

"Thanks, Ma."

Logan wrapped a dishcloth around the hot jar. Tess opened the kitchen door for him. The sound of peepers drifted in with the night air as he stepped outside and gently set the jar on the ground.

I have the best family, he thought.

CHAPTER 8

THE NEWSPAPER OFFICE

Lightning's hooves clip-clopped against cobblestones as the Pryces' buggy turned onto Main Street. It was a warm Saturday afternoon, and many people were out and about doing their errands.

Logan sat next to Pa and held on to his finished wheel. He had completed his repairs on schedule.

He had even painted the whole thing blue, his favorite color. He had found an old dried-up tin of paint in his Fix-It Shop and mixed in some vinegar and milk to make it usable again. Now all he had to do was convince Mr. Mayberry to buy the wheel.

"We're almost there," Pa told Logan as he steered the buggy.

"I need to stop by the newspaper office so I can pick up my pay. We'll go over to the general store right after."

"Yes, Pa."

"You did a nice job on your wheel, son."

"Thanks, Pa."

"Here we are!" Pa tugged on the reins, and Lightning slowed her pace.

They stopped in front of a tall brick building. A sign in the window read THE MAPLE RIDGE MESSENGER.

Pa tied Lightning's reins to a hitching post and headed inside.

Logan followed, carrying his wheel.

A young woman sat behind a desk. "Good afternoon, Mr. Pryce. Mr. Dawson is working in the back. He's expecting you," she called out.

"Thank you, Miss Mosely."

They found Mr. Dawson in a large room filled with boxes, crates, and paper. He was a tall man with gray hair and round spectacles.

Mr. Dawson shook Pa's hand and then Logan's. Logan grinned and felt very grown-up.

Mr. Dawson pointed to a big machine in the middle of the room. It had belts, levers, rollers, and a motor, too. "How do you like my

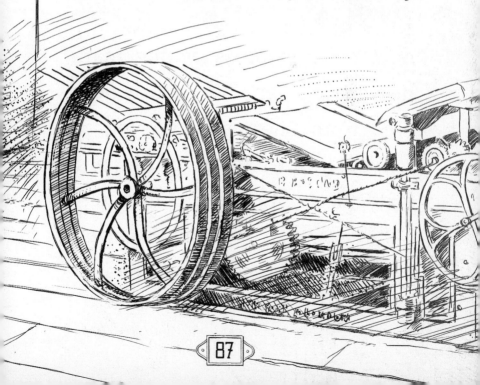

new printing press, young man?"
he asked Logan. "We had it deliv-
ered from Sherman, and your pa
helped me set it up. It can print
sixty sheets of paper per minute!"

"That's swell!"
Logan gushed.

Mr. Dawson eyed Logan's wheel curiously. "What do you have there?"

"It's a buggy wheel, sir!" Logan said, standing up very straight. "I found it by the side of the road. I fixed it up and painted it. I'm hoping to sell it to Mr. Mayberry. Our school needs the money for repairs."

"Is that so? What

kind of repairs?" asked Mr. Dawson.

Logan told the whole story to Mr. Dawson. When he had finished, Mr. Dawson looked thoughtful. "Hmm. That would make an interesting article for my first issue of the *Messenger*. Would you mind if I quoted you, young man?"

Logan's jaw dropped. Mr. Dawson wanted to quote him, Logan Pryce, in a newspaper article?

Logan turned to Pa. Pa smiled and nodded.

This is my lucky day! Logan thought, hugging the wheel to his chest.

CHAPTER 9

A SURPRISING CUSTOMER

After their visit with Mr. Dawson, Logan and Pa headed over to Mayberry's General Store. Logan carried his wheel. Pa carried a basket filled with Ma's homemade goods, for trading.

A tiny bell jingled as Logan and Pa entered the store. Mrs. Mayberry was at the counter, cutting a bolt of

white linen for a customer.

"Why, hello there, Pryces!" Mrs. Mayberry said cheerfully. "Where's your ma, Logan? She usually comes in on Saturdays with butter and jam for me."

"Alice and the girls took some soup over to Mrs. Gruen. Poor woman's been feeling under the weather. I brought the butter and jam this time." Pa held up his basket. "She wants to know if she can get some coffee, salt, and sugar in exchange."

"Happy to oblige," said Mrs. Mayberry.

"Is Mr. Mayberry here?" asked Logan.

"He's in his office going over his books. You can go on back," Mrs. Mayberry told him.

Logan started down the crowded aisle, being careful not to knock down anything with his wheel. He passed drawers full of spices, bins piled high with apples, and shelves stocked with pots and pans. He loved the store, which sold everything from groceries to tools. It was also a gathering place. People sat around and played checkers or caught up on one another's news. They could get their mail there too, or use the telephone to call out of town.

Mr. Mayberry was in his office, leafing through a fat brown ledger. "Why, hello there, Logan! Have you come to see me about something?"

"Yes, sir. I'm here to sell you my wheel!" Logan announced grandly.

"Oh?" Mr. Mayberry squinted at the wheel. "I've never seen a blue buggy wheel before. Are the other three blue as well?"

"Actually, there is only this one wheel," Logan admitted. "I found it by the side of the road and repaired it in my Fix-It Shop. I thought you could resell it to one of your customers for a profit."

"I see." Mr. Mayberry stroked his moustache. "I wish I could help you, Logan. But I can't use just one wheel. My customers want sets of four, you see."

Logan blinked. A sick feeling washed over him. He had counted on Mr. Mayberry to buy his wheel for forty cents. His plan was falling apart!

"Excuse me." A large man with a bushy beard stood in the doorway. His gray suit and gold-tipped cane looked fancy and expensive.

Mr. Mayberry jumped up from his chair. "Why . . . Mr. Bird! I didn't realize you were here. It's a pleasure to see you, sir. Can I help you with something?"

Mr. Bird? Logan remembered that name well. Pa had worked at Mayberry's a few weeks back. Logan had come in to help, only to cause a big mix-up with Mr. Bird's special order.

Mr. Bird pointed to Logan's wheel. "Did I hear you say that item is for sale?" he asked.

"Y-yes, yes, sir," Logan replied, confused.

"Well, then, I would very much

like to buy it for my wife," Mr. Bird declared.

Mr. Mayberry gasped in surprise. Logan broke into a huge smile.

"Mrs. Bird likes to put ornaments in her flower garden. That wheel

would make a fine ornament. Also, blue is her favorite color," Mr. Bird explained.

He reached into the pocket of his fancy gray suit. He handed a few coins to Logan. "Would seventy-five cents be enough? No, let's make it an even dollar, shall we?"

A dollar? Logan could give fifty cents to the school and still have fifty cents left over for his piggy

bank. And he wouldn't have to use Tess's and Drew's nickels, after all.

Today was definitely Logan's lucky day!

CHAPTER 10

THE FIX-IT PARTY

Logan had never seen so many people in their schoolhouse.

It seemed as though half of Maple Ridge had gathered to pitch in with the repairs. All the students and their families were there. Many of the Pryces' neighbors were there. Even the mayor of Maple Ridge was there.

Big swaths of cloth covered the desks and bookshelves. The steady din of saws and hammers filled the room. Drew helped Mr. Bruna put the new windowpane in place. Annie and Tess helped Ma sweep up the fallen plaster. Logan helped Pa replace one of the floorboards.

Miss Ashley came up to Logan, carrying a bucket. Bits of plaster and paint clung to her blond hair. "This wonderful turn-out is all because of you, Logan," she praised him.

"Me? What did I do?" Logan asked, surprised.

"Oh, my goodness! I guess you haven't seen this yet," replied Miss Ashley.

She reached into her smock and handed Logan a newspaper. Logan glanced at the front page. It was the first edition of the Maple Ridge Messenger.

THE MESSENGER

MAPLE RIDGE

A big headline read CHILDREN RAISE MONEY FOR SCHOOL REPAIRS.

The article went on to explain that the school had needed repairs for a long time. It quoted Logan at

the end: "I fixed up an old buggy wheel. I plan to sell it so I can give the money to my school."

SSENGER

RIDGE

CHILDREN RAISE MONEY FOR SCHOOL REPAIRS

Maple Ridge School needs more

than just a lick of whitewash!

Floors, walls, ceiling and windows

all need repairing. The pupils at

Ridge school have managed

money to get the

"A lot of the folks in Maple Ridge read this article," said Miss Ashley. "That's why we have so many volunteers here today."

"I'm proud of you, son," Pa told him.

"Thanks, Pa. And thanks, Miss Ashley!" Logan said happily.

As they got back to work, Logan wiped his brow and peered around the room. Even with the sawdust and plaster everywhere—and even with the repairs half finished—he could picture how fine the school was going to look. And he was glad that he was a part of it. This was surely his biggest and most important fix-it project ever!

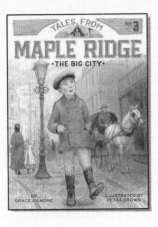

Check out the next

TALES FROM MAPLE RIDGE

adventure!

HERE'S A SNEAK PEEK!

Logan Pryce dipped his net into the pond and swished it through the water.

"Got you!" he shouted.

He reached into the net and pulled out a fat green frog. It wiggled out of his fist and hopped back into the pond with a loud splash!

Next to Logan, his best friend, Anthony Bruna, laughed. "Gosh,

that's the sixth frog that's gotten away from you today."

Logan grinned. "Oh, well! I'm bored of catching frogs anyway."

"Bored? But you love catching frogs."

"Maybe when I was seven. That was a long time ago."

"What do you want to do now?" asked Anthony. "Go fishing in the creek? Walk over to the general store? I think I have a penny to buy candy." He dug through his dungaree pockets.

"I should probably pack for my big trip," said Logan.

TALES FROM
MAPLE RIDGE

Find excerpts, activities, and more at
TalesfromMapleRidge.com!